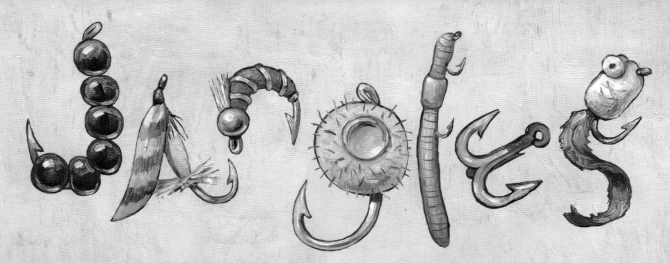

Jangles

a **BIG** fish story

by
DAVID
SHANNON

THE BLUE SKY PRESS • AN IMPRINT OF SCHOLASTIC INC. • NEW YORK

To Roger, Gregor, Adam, Jonrad, Buzz, Bob, Gino "Comply," Tom "Be-the-Fly,"
the Baldecchi Brothers, Doc, Doug, Peck, Rafe, Hazlett, Hemingway, and
all the other liars and storytellers I may or may not have fished with.

THE BLUE SKY PRESS

Library of Congress catalog card number: 2012006173   ISBN 978-0-545-14312-7

10 9 8 7 6 5 4 3 2 1   12 13 14 15 16

Printed in China   38   First printing, October 2012

Designed by David Shannon and Kathleen Westray

WHEN THE SUN goes down and the weather's just right,
Big Lake gets smooth as glass and a thin mist whispers across it.
That's when you might catch a glimpse of Jangles.

My father told me lots of stories, but my favorite was about a
giant trout he saw when he was a kid. I still remember sitting with
him in front of the big stone fireplace at the cabin. He pulled out
a dirty green tackle box and shook it a couple times so it rattled.
Then he told me this story. . . .

When I was a kid, Jangles was the biggest fish anyone had ever seen—or heard! That's right, you could *hear* Jangles. He'd broken so many fishing lines that his huge, crooked jaw was covered with shiny metal lures and rusty old fishhooks of all shapes and sizes. They clinked and clattered as he swam. That's why he was called Jangles.

Jangles was so big, he ate eagles from the trees that hung out over the lake and full-grown beavers that strayed too far from home.

But he didn't seem to care much for the taste of kids. In fact, people swear one time Jangles saved a baby who fell into the lake when his family's canoe tipped over. They say he took that baby up so gently that none of the hooks even stuck it, and he swam it to shore. Supposedly he gave the baby's momma a dirty look as if to say, *What are you doing bringing your precious little baby out here in a tippy old canoe?!*

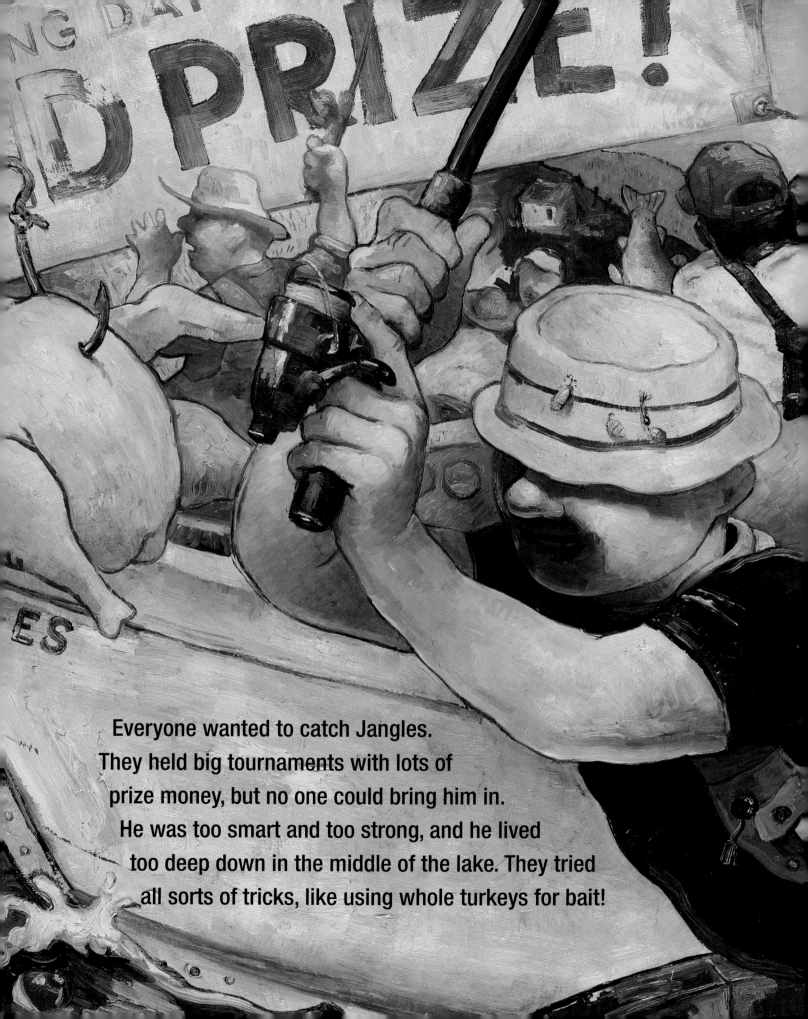

Everyone wanted to catch Jangles.
They held big tournaments with lots of
prize money, but no one could bring him in.
He was too smart and too strong, and he lived
too deep down in the middle of the lake. They tried
all sorts of tricks, like using whole turkeys for bait!

One fellow even tried dynamite. He threw
big cans of tuna fish in the water and waited till
he heard Jangles coming. Then he lit a stick of dynamite
and tossed it in the lake. I don't know if it hit a rock or something,

but that dynamite came flying back out of the water
and into his boat and blew it to smithereens! Then he
had to swim all the way back to his dock. He said Jangles
came up and bumped him on his butt, but nobody believed him.

One time when I was just about your age, I was fishing over where the creek comes into the lake, and my anchor came loose. I was concentrating so hard on catching a fish that I didn't notice I was drifting way out into the middle of the lake. There wasn't another soul out there, and it was getting dark.

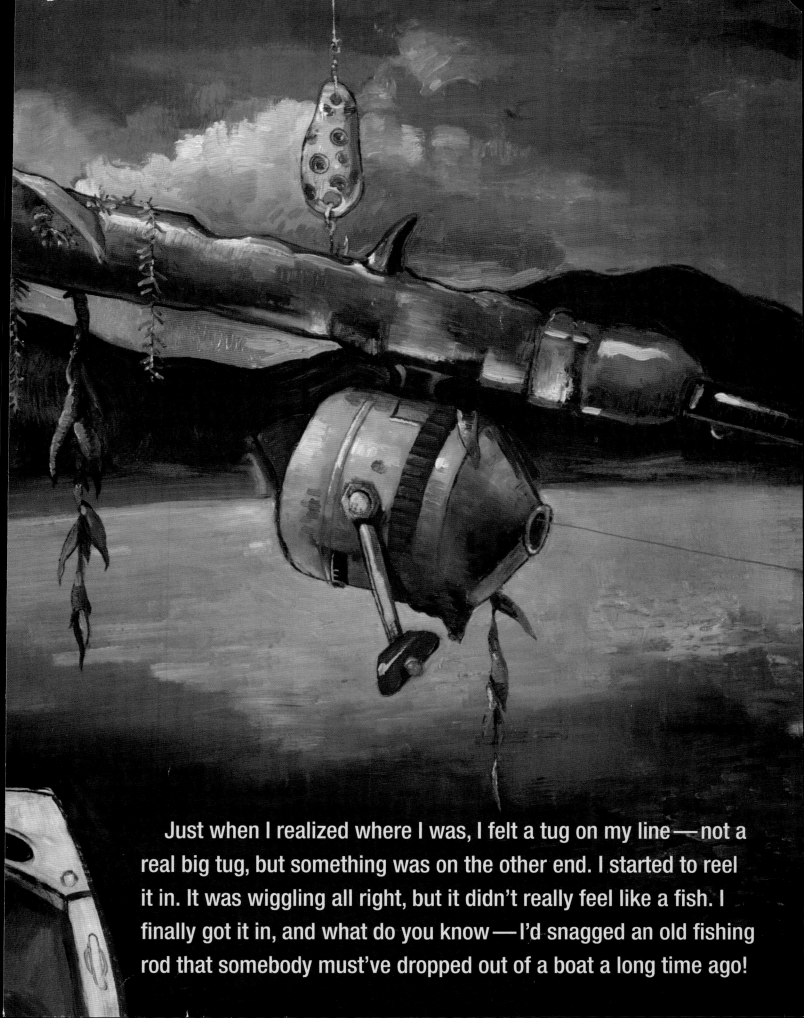

Just when I realized where I was, I felt a tug on my line—not a real big tug, but something was on the other end. I started to reel it in. It was wiggling all right, but it didn't really feel like a fish. I finally got it in, and what do you know—I'd snagged an old fishing rod that somebody must've dropped out of a boat a long time ago!

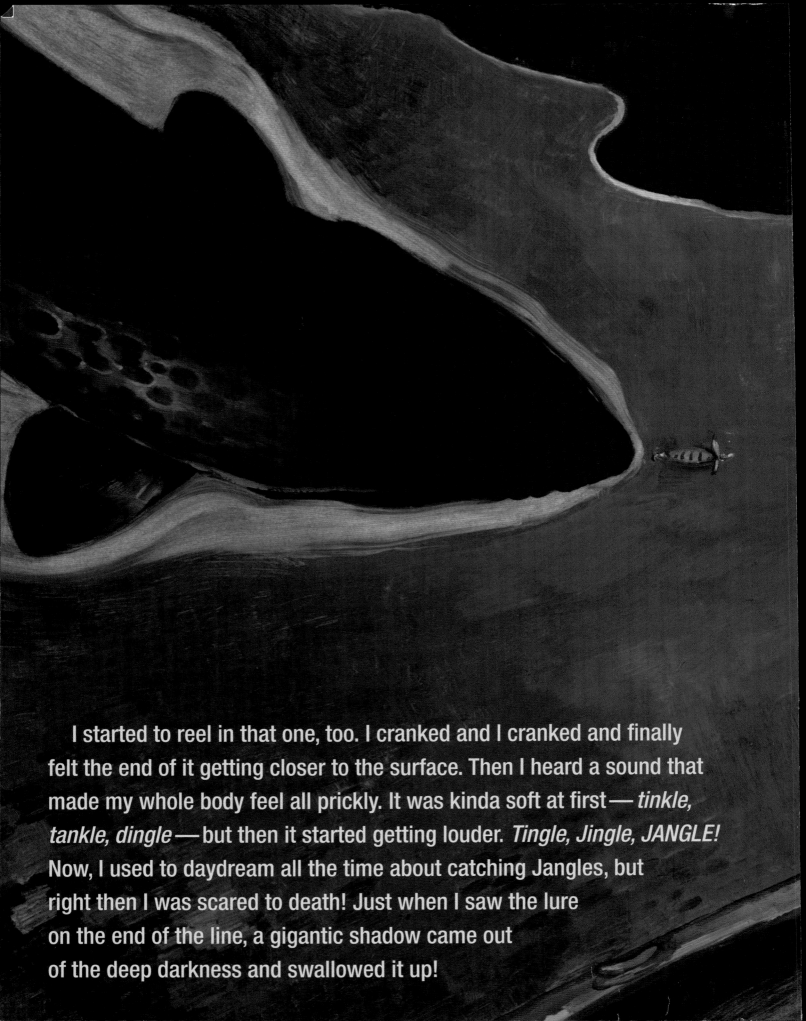

I started to reel in that one, too. I cranked and I cranked and finally
felt the end of it getting closer to the surface. Then I heard a sound that
made my whole body feel all prickly. It was kinda soft at first — *tinkle,
tankle, dingle* — but then it started getting louder. *Tingle, Jingle, JANGLE!*
Now, I used to daydream all the time about catching Jangles, but
right then I was scared to death! Just when I saw the lure
on the end of the line, a gigantic shadow came out
of the deep darkness and swallowed it up!

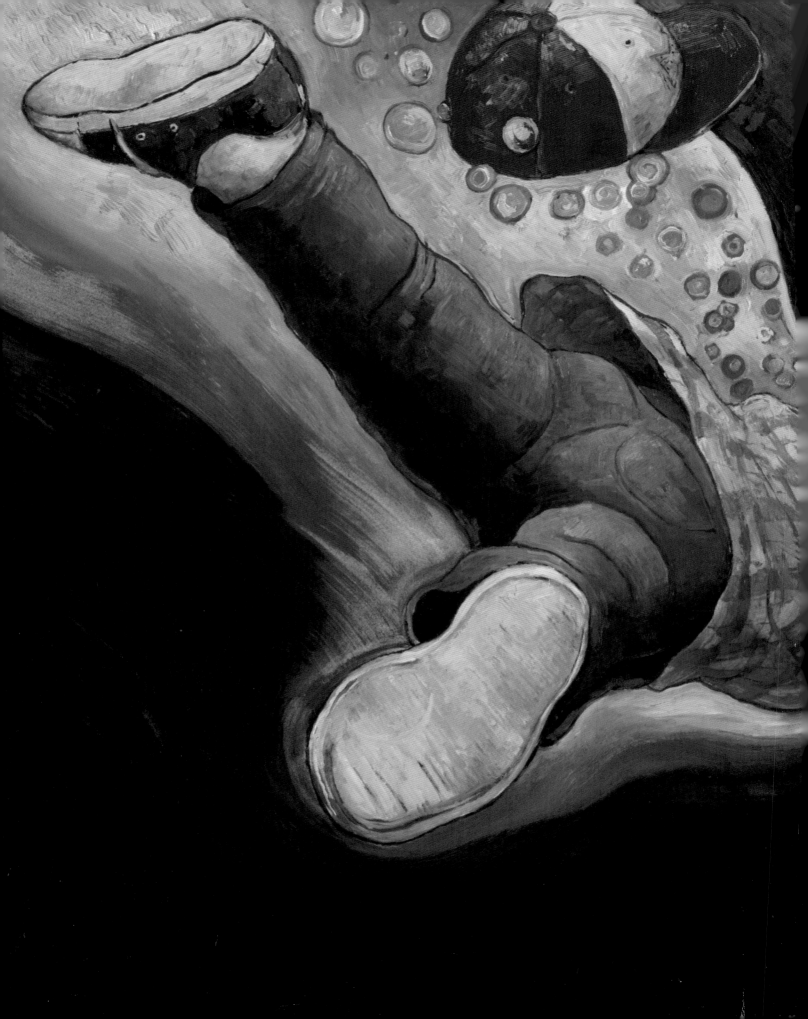

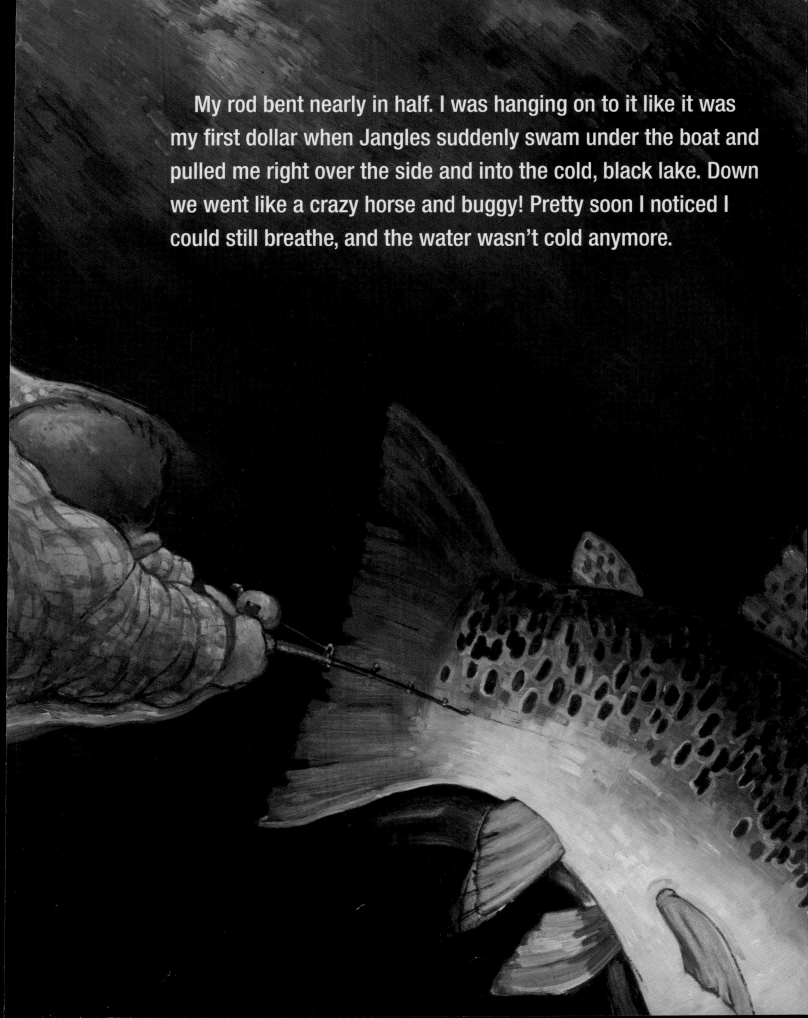

My rod bent nearly in half. I was hanging on to it like it was my first dollar when Jangles suddenly swam under the boat and pulled me right over the side and into the cold, black lake. Down we went like a crazy horse and buggy! Pretty soon I noticed I could still breathe, and the water wasn't cold anymore.

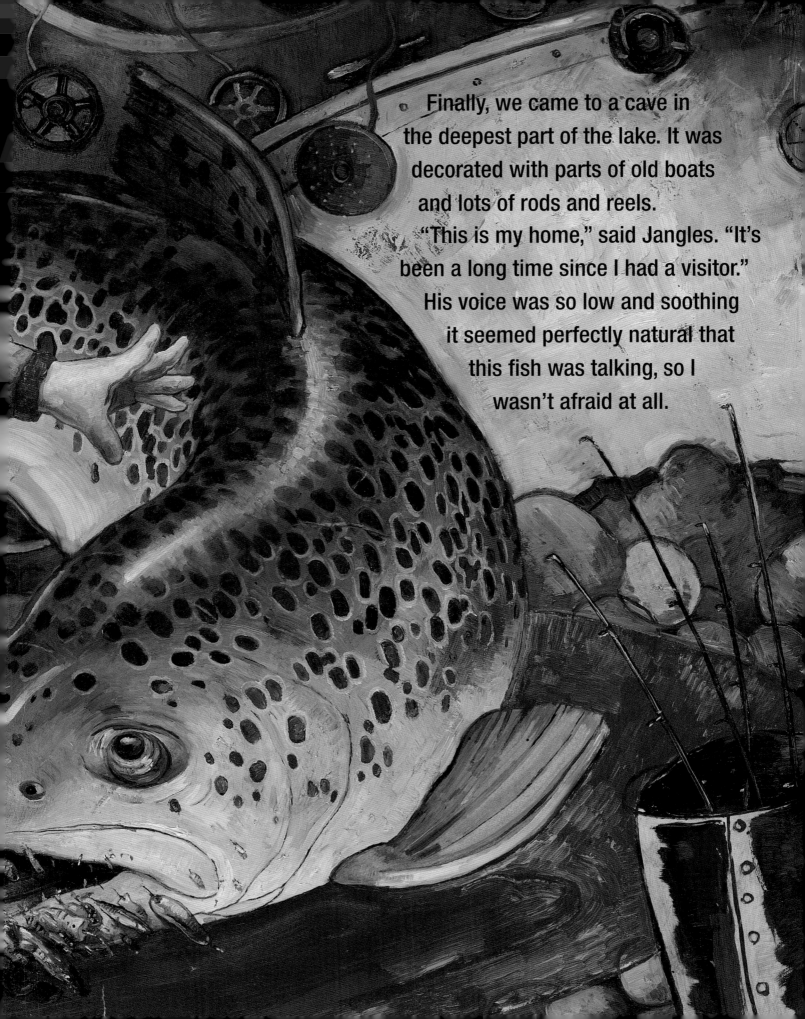

Finally, we came to a cave in the deepest part of the lake. It was decorated with parts of old boats and lots of rods and reels.

"This is my home," said Jangles. "It's been a long time since I had a visitor."

His voice was so low and soothing it seemed perfectly natural that this fish was talking, so I wasn't afraid at all.

Then Jangles told me stories. Amazing, wonderful stories about the beginning of the Earth before there were people, and stories about wise old redwood trees and animals who were silly and the great fish that lived before him in Big Lake. It was like Jangles was my magic uncle! After a while I started to get sleepy, and he said, "Time to go."

He told me to hang on to the big fin on his back. I still had the old rod in my hand, and as we swam up and the water turned from black to purple, I slowly pulled out some line and made a bunch of long loops. When we reached the surface, Jangles swam alongside my boat. Quick as a minnow, I hopped off the fish's giant back and threw the coils of line around him. Then, with a sharp yank, I spun him upside down!

Now, you might not know this, but when you turn a fish upside down—even a big, old, smart fish like Jangles—it gets confused and can't hardly move. Like it's paralyzed.

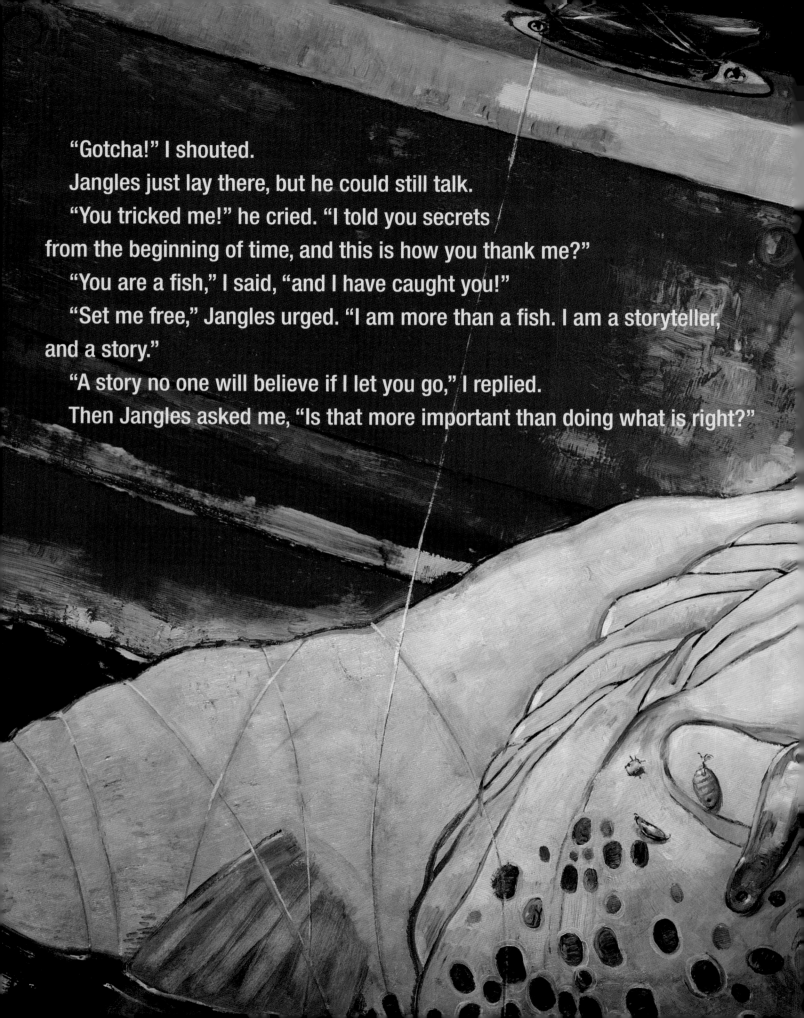

"Gotcha!" I shouted.

Jangles just lay there, but he could still talk.

"You tricked me!" he cried. "I told you secrets from the beginning of time, and this is how you thank me?"

"You are a fish," I said, "and I have caught you!"

"Set me free," Jangles urged. "I am more than a fish. I am a storyteller, and a story."

"A story no one will believe if I let you go," I replied.

Then Jangles asked me, "Is that more important than doing what is right?"

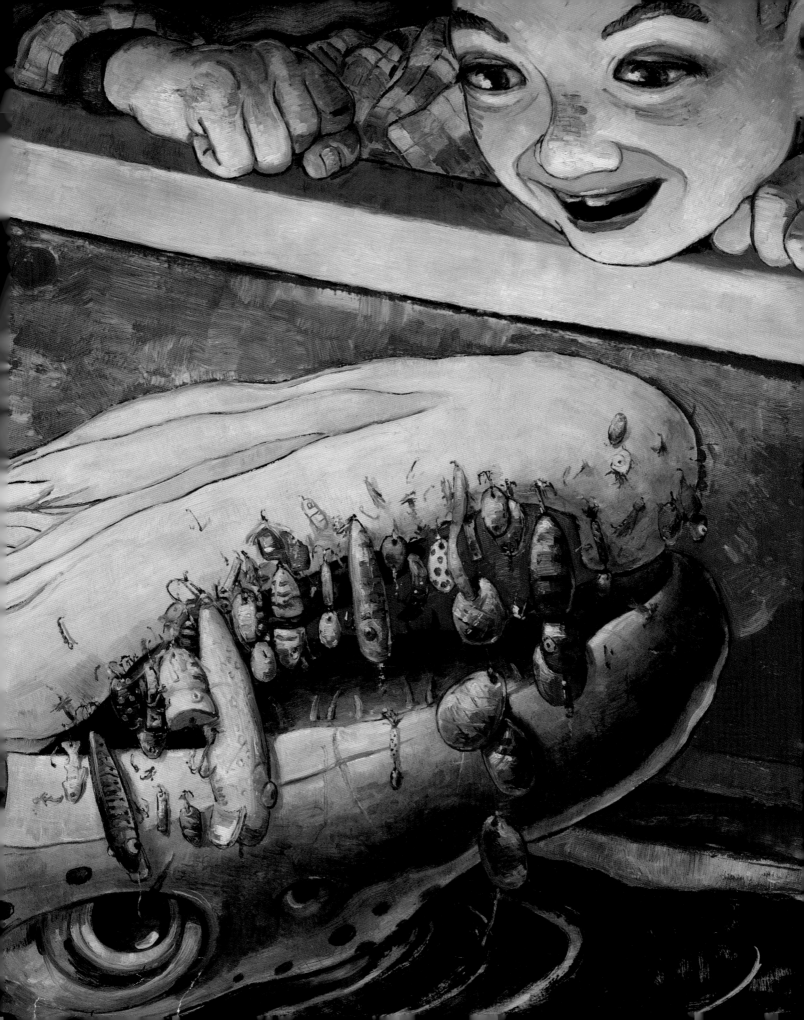

I thought of all the wondrous things I'd heard that day. Then I thought about people dragging whole turkeys around the lake. "You're right," I said. "I'm sorry. I will set you free, but what can I do to apologize?"

I swear Jangles grinned at me with that big, crooked, jingly jaw of his. "There is one thing you can do to help me," he said, "and it would also prove you caught ol' Jangles. . . ."

That's when my dad stopped telling his story and gave me his tackle box. It was full to the top with shiny metal lures and rusty old fishhooks of all shapes and sizes. He never told anyone about catching the giant fish. He kept it a secret until that night when he told me.

And now I'm telling you.